CW00821081

ROTTEN, MOULDY, MUSIC

A Story for Humorous Children

ROBERT BLANCHETT

Copyright © 2016 ROBERT BLANCHETT

All rights reserved.

ISBN: **1532718969**
ISBN-13: 978-1532718960

DEDICATION

For Stanley John Keet
and
Teddy Alexander Keet

CONTENTS

1 How to Play a Saxophone

You know me, I'm Anthony. I'm the one with the pesky little brother Daniel and the bossy big sister who calls herself Emma.

I call her Em. It stands for Mad.

Em often asks us, "Do you know what Em stands for? My name's Em, M for Madwoman."

Dan calls her 'Em For'.

I don't know why, but in our family nobody can keep their real name for long enough to know how to spell it.

I was six years old before I found out I was supposed to tell teachers and doctors and such-like that my real name is Anthony (which is what nobody else calls me), not Ant. And what a stupid name to try to spell!

It doesn't make any kind of sense!

Did you guess that my big sister Em – that's M for Madwoman – drew my face on this picture for me? What do you think? The face is mouldy! I'm going to draw ALL of the next picture of us in the shop MYSELF. Hands off my pictures! That includes you, Dan!

I was in this shop with Dan, a.k.a. (a.k.a. means, "Also Known to Old people As") Daniel. We had been taken there by our Mum, of course.

The one we call Em for Madwoman was staying at home. She was looking after the cat. She said the cat would be lonely without her, but really she only likes to buy clothes from special shops. Mum told her in that if she stayed behind she would have to do some revising.

No one has ever caught Em doing anything other than sitting curled up in a warm armchair reading an adventure book and eating a chocolate bar while she's revising. No one has ever found out what this 'revising' stuff is.

We just know what it looks like.

Dracula

Choc bar

Dracula Book

bars

arm Chair

Em doing her science revision

I have never, ever, had horrible pigtails like that. Not since I was 4, or 9, or something.
Emma B.

Our favourite shop is a charity shop. Em calls it, 'your junk shop.' She says she can't understand why we have to go there, it's full of other people's old clothes. It's stuff they don't want to be seen dead in, walking about wearing it. Er?

Mum says, "Emma is becoming quite the fashionable young madam." No one knows what that means.

Mum likes to rummage in the shop. She tries to find, "Something unusual and out of the ordinary." That stuff is out of the ordinary alright.

We were at the back. We had walked in past all the old children's books with ice cream stains down the front and cooked bacon slices stuck inside as bookmarks. We wanted to look in them to see what we could find, but this time we weren't allowed.

Next to the smelly old shoes, we were supposed to be looking at the toys. Mum had said we could buy a jigsaw, but Em says that all the jigsaws in that place are mouldy. They always have one or two pieces missing that the owners lost when they were putting a fat old elastic band round the box.

According to Dan, a dog ate the missing pieces. Because the dog ate the pieces, they didn't want the jigsaw anymore and gave it to charity, with however many pieces were left.

Mum is always cross about that, because she says all the pieces are there at the start but we always manage to lose some.

I think that Dan is right: a dog ate them.

Very quickly, in amongst the smelly shoes and boots, there's my little brother, Old Dan, with his head inside something interesting.

I'm sorry folks, but I had to get my big sister Em to draw the golden brass thingy for me. Also, she drew Daniel. But I did draw the bench thingy going up hill with the shoes on it. What do you think of the shoes? Pretty cool drawing, eh?

"What is that, Dan?" I asked him.

Good question? He couldn't see me with his head stuck in that thing, but I'm sure he could hear me, because he started shouting: "Er humphh, bah berumph!"

"What was that you just said Dan?!"

"Er humphh, bah berumph!"

That's what it sounded like he said, because he'd got his head inside this really big, metal thing.

"What's in there?"

"Cerr humphh, bah berumph!" he answered.

I pushed him out of the way and stuck my head in. I couldn't see anything interesting. In fact, I couldn't see anything at all. It was gold outside but it sure was dark in there.

"Ooj kump ber hmm bennychung!" I shouted at him from inside the thing.

Suddenly, I felt something crawling on my neck. I jumped up and hit my head on the metal thing.

It was my Mum's hand on my collar.

"What ARE you doing, looking in that saxophone?" she asked.

"I was just looking to see how you turn it on. They've lost the instructions," I explained to her.

"Instructions?"

Funny, isn't it, how parents love to repeat what you just said? They turn it into a question and make it sound like YOU are the mad one.

Dan was fiddling about with the big, gold-coloured thing, pulling out little circular bits and trying to get them to flip back. Mum seemed to

be getting agitated, just because
other people in the shop had all
stopped what they were doing and
were staring at us.

Dan's drawing of, of
every one looking at
us. (It's hard writing on
plain paper. I'm going to
get some with a liner

With one hand, she pulled Dan away while still smiling at everyone. Somehow she made it look like she was happy and gentle. She made it seem like this is the kind of thing we do to each other all the time in our family, just as soon as we get the chance.

Unfortunately, Dan was clinging on for dear life to the shiny thing and it started to come off the shelf as Mum pulled him away. With her other hand, Mum managed to pull the brass golden thing away from Dan and swung it back onto the shelf.

Neat trick Mum!

"Now you two, just what do you think you're doing?"

We looked at each other. We each pulled a face. ERM? What's she on about now?

At last Mum gave in and explained. "It's an instrument. You CAN'T turn it on, you have to blow into it."

"An instrument!" Dan bellowed. "What's the INSTRUMENT done to me? Is it a doctor's *instrument*?"

"What? Does it look like a doctor's instrument?"

That's another thing about adults: they ask questions that have absolutely no sense at all! The thing didn't look like anything, and she had just told us that it was an instrument, so why ask us if it looked like one? I mean, mad or what?

And another thing, just how many kinds of instruments are there?

"Musical; it's a musical instrument! You blow down it. It's called a saxophone. Now you two, leave it alone and let me get on with looking at these clothes. I've just seen a lovely jumper for you, Ant."

We stood looking at each other. We had been told to leave it alone. Dan cracked first. I knew that he would.

Dan slid across to the saxo thing, put his head back down the wide end again, and blew as hard as he could.

It hardly made a little phart noise.

There's a special thing one of the boys at school taught us. You put your hands together and squeeze, to warm them up. When you have got your hands nice and sweaty, you capture some air inside and squeeze carefully. I decided it was the right time to warm my hands up.

How to do a hand squeak with
your hands.

1. Look at your ~~left right left~~
both hands. Like this

fingers

thumb

thumb

3 Salt of turn them together ~~flat~~ against
(What the poor little twerp is trying to
say is, "Put your palms together." Emma)
4. Kind of turn ~~the~~ your hands across

fingers

right thumb

left

5. Kind of squeeze them until
get hot and sweaty. Pump with hot hands
6. Squeeze gently to make a noise
+ Play a tune by changing the
squeeze.

21

I knew my hands were just right. The sound came out high at first, in little squeaks, and then developed into a much longer noise:

"Pheeeeeeeeeeeeeeeeeeeeeeeeeii iiiiiiieeeeeeeeeeeeeeeeeeeeeaaaaa aaaaaaareeeeeeeeeeeeeeeeiiiieeeee eeeeeeeeart."

We were back in the car faster than you could ask, "What are you two doing? I thought I told you..."

Back in Mum's car
faster than you coun
ask "What do you
two think you are
doing?"

2 The Mad Way to Buy a Musical Instrument

Much later. Or was it a bit later?

Just after.

"Dan, we need you to ask Em how to get enough money to buy the saxo thing."

"Er?"

That's the thing about Dan, he doesn't do that adult thingy about asking the same question back. He's much more sensible than that. He just says, "Er?"

I pushed him upstairs, knocked on Em for Madwoman's door,

opened it, and pushed him in. When he didn't come flying back out again, I sneaked in.

"Get out of here, punks!" Em screamed from her chair.

Why hadn't she shouted at Dan? I bet he just stood there, grinning.

"I'll give you a count of ten. After that, this chocolate bar will be molten and useless. I won't want it if it's melted, will I? I'll push it in your grubby little faces! Now, GET OUT!"

Dan jumped backwards into me, so I pushed him hard back, right in front of the M woman.

"Em For," Dan began. Then he stopped until I dug him in the ribs. "Em For, how can we get lots of money and buy an instrument thing that doctors use to stick your head in, to... to make you feel better?"

M woman stared with the chocolate bar stuck halfway in her mouth.

"What are you two on? No one knows what meaningless words will come out of your mouths next!"

"How can we get lots of money and buy an instrument thing that doctors use to stick your head in, to... to make you feel better?" Dan repeated.

"How am I supposed to get on with my revision when every few minutes I'm interrupted by you two morons?"

It was best not to say anything. The safest thing would be to keep absolutely silent. Always keep your lips tightly shut at times like that.

I answered: "We couldn't have been interrupting every few minutes, because we were out with Mum. We were shopping, for a saxophone."

Dan can be very quick. He ducked and the wet and soggy chocolate bar hit me on the chest.

"Emma!" I shouted. "Now I've got chocolate on it! It's all down my brand new jumper!"

"Did you get that in your junk shop? It might have been brand new for the boy who had it before you. It *looked* brand new, at least it did before you got chocolate all over it, you messy pup, but really it's one that's already been worn by the boy whose Mum took it to the junk shop. Just you remember that."

We were halfway down the stairs when she called us back.

"I've got an idea", she said. "Make lots of donuts and sell them. People love donuts. You can sell them to the neighbours, and to your friends, and their mothers."

"And their dogs," added Dan.

"But, for every pound you make, you will have to give me 25 pence."

"What for?"

"For having the big idea. It's called 'commission'. And because if you don't give it me, I'll make your life very unpleasant."

"It's already unpleasant," I said.

"Can we have the donuts without the commish... the commishshshsh..." Dan tried.

"Not if you don't want to find something nasty - such as a half-eaten bar of chocolate - stuck in your bed one night, you can't."

We knew what was coming next.

"What does M stand for?"

"Madwoman."

"That's right. Just you remember it."

3 Find the Instrument

When we were safely back downstairs, I asked Dan for his opinion. That means, I asked him what to do next. It's always best to ask him, because if anything goes wrong we all know who to blame.

"Let's go and stand in the kitchen," Dan suggested.

"What for, Dan?"

"Because... Because... Because you asked me to."

"No I didn't!"

"Yes you did. You asked me what to do next. I heard you."

"I didn't hear you."

"Yes you did! You asked me what to do next. I heard you."

I decided to stop saying anything. Dan can keep that kind of thing up forever.

We stood in the kitchen for quite a long while. It was boring. You can't look in any of the cupboards, because my Mum put special catches on them when we were babies. She put the catches on to stop us looking in the cupboards. Then she forgot to take them off when we grew bigger. We told her we wouldn't want to look in the cupboards now that we weren't babies and she could take the catches off again, but she said she had better things to do. That's made it boring, because now we still can't look inside them.

Our Mum came in and asked just what I knew she would ask.

I won't bore you by telling you what she asked. Also, it's much shorter and quicker if I don't tell you what she asked, because I bet you can guess what she said. Of course, you might not be very good at guessing and get it wrong. (What she said, you could get that wrong. You might NOT get it wrong, but you still could, if you don't know my Mum.) But look at it this way, it's still best to do it like this and not explain what she asked, because all the kids who do know what she would ask would get bored while I explained to anyone who got it wrong, or to anyone who couldn't think what she would say. This way, it's much, much quicker for everyone.

"Emma told us we've got to make some donuts," I answered.

"Emma said you've got to make some donuts?"

That was what I had just told her, so I didn't say anything else. I don't know why she had forgotten that I had just told her that Emma said it.

"Why have you 'got to' make some?"

"We want sell them to make a lot of money and buy the saxo thing," Old Dan told her.

"Saxo? How would selling salt...? Oh, you mean the saxophone! It's much too expensive and far too big for you."

"It's for Ant. I didn't like the tune when I blew into the big, gold bit."

Well, you can guess, that just reminded Mum and we got told off again. At last she decided that we could go back to the shop and see for ourselves.

"Just a minute!" she shouted. "What's this awful sticky mess on your new jersey?"

"It's not new," I said. "I found out from *someone,* that *someone else* has worn it already."

"It was Em!" Dan shouted.

"Emma wore your jersey? Whatever for? How did she get it on? She might have stretched it! Did she even get it over her head, I wonder?"

"She didn't get it over her head," I answered truthfully.

I had to go and try to wash the front of my jersey. When I got in the car, I had a horrible, wet, chocolate smudge all down the front of the mouldy old jersey that someone else had already worn.

When we got in the shop, Mum stood the saxophone next to me.

Emma drew the saxo
thing. I did me.

The shop lady came over to ask if she could help.

"Oh, what a shame!" she said. "You've got something on your new jersey already. Your mother's not going to be very pleased with you, is she?"

"It wasn't me!" Dan shouted.

"Did I tell you that the jersey was brand new? The lady who brought it in told me she had bought it for her grandson, but when he came to see her, she realised she had forgotten just how tall he was, so he didn't even try it on. Aren't you pleased with it? When it's washed it will look lovely again."

"Well?" said Mum.

"Well what, Mum?"

"What do you say?"

"Can we buy one of the jigsaws, please?"

Mum told the lady why we were playing around with the instrument.

The lady went into another room and came out with a guitar and a thing called a tuning-fork.

"One tuning-fork is no good," she told us.

She placed the fork thing on a bench. Then she told us the guitar needed some strings and there was something wrong with the piece she called the neck. Because it was broken, she said Mum could have it for free, to see if she could mend it. Otherwise the lady was going to throw the broken instrument away.

Everyone was happy. Mum said thank you. Then Dan spoilt it all. He dropped the tuning-fork and it broke. He said he was trying to play a tune on it, because the lady said it was a tune fork.

The kind lady said it didn't matter, but Mum shouted at us. She said we mustn't touch anything.

Emma says I must try to do joined up writing from now on. She did this mouldy drawing of me not touching anything. Dan said, "Whooo! Ant's got a ghost! It's behind you!"

"What are you doing now?" she shouted. She shouted just because we were standing with our hands up in the air.

"You said we mustn't touch anything!"

Soon we were back in the car before you could say something... AGAIN!

Back in Mum's car faster than you can ask "What do you two think you are doing?"

4. Meet My Sister, Madwoman

We ran straight back upstairs to Emma's room when we got back. She was still revising the vampire-lover book.

"Em," I shouted, "I don't need to pay you any commish thing now. Mum's got me a guitar!"

"Don't you dare come gloating in my room without knocking!" she bellowed.

"What's gloating?" Dan asked.

"It's something that's not wanted in this house!"

We tried to think what might not be wanted in our house.

Not Wanted

My sister Em for Madwoman.
~~Subscanshatts~~ very big reward
for keeping her at your house and
not bringing her back.

"Don't just stand there gawping,
get out of here. Just remember, Em
stands for Madwoman..."

"What does A stand for?" Dan
asked.

Em looked a bit bewildered, but she sees it as her role to teach us a thing or two.

"Do you mean Anthony?"

"What does B stand for?"

"We don't know ANYONE whose name begins with B."

"What does C stand for?"

"Eek, the little twerp's going through the alphabet! Stop him Ant!"

"What does D stand for?"

"Mum!" yelled Em. "Daniel's doing some really weird alphabet thing! Come and make him shut up!"

"What does E stand for?"

"Mum, he's freaking me out!"

"What does F stand for?"

"MUM! YOU'VE GOT TO COME QUICK!"

"What does G stand for?"

Mum appeared at the doorway.

"What does H stand for?"

"Quick Mum, you've got to do something! Dan's driving us insane!"

"What does I stand for?"

"Em, we really don't need all that fuss! He's nearly at the end of the alphabet, and then he'll stop, won't he."

"What does J stand for?"

"No he won't," I said, helpfully.

"What does K stand for?"

"When he gets to Z, he'll start all over again, at A."

"What does L stand for?"

"I can't stand it!" Em yelled, putting her hands over her ears.

"What does M stand for?"

"Give me a chance!" Mum said, sternly. "You only just asked about L. L stands for Livorno."

"What does M stand for?"

"M is for Milano."

"What does N stand for?"

"Napoli."

"What does O stand for?"

"Orvieto."

"Er?"

"Hurrah!" Em and I both cheered.

"At last the little weirdo's stopped. Thanks Mum, but if you don't mind, I think I'd like to move out and go and live at the zoo. It would be a lot more normal in there."

Emma in her new home at the zoo

What I did was, I asked Emma to draw a lion for me on a clean sheet of paper.

Mum patted Dan on the head and went back downstairs.

"How did you know he wouldn't stop at Z?" Em asked me. "Has he done this before?"

"No," I answered. "I just... sort of... thought it."

"Idiot! Now get out of my room, before I turn you both into zombies!"

I pushed Dan out the door, ready to run for it, but she called us back.

"Wait a minute though! Come in here and I'll explain something to your pea brains. If you want to keep the money, you could give me 5 donuts for every 10 you make. That's after you two have tasted some first, to prove that they're not poisoned. And you will have to change that jersey before you start baking: it's got messy chocolate all down the front, you horribly messy little zombie."

5 Bazooka

I was sitting in an armchair holding
my tennis racket up in the trigger
position, waiting for a mosquito to
come in. My tennis teacher had told
me I had got to practise my smash.

Dan was eating some kind of
little orange thing he had found in a
bowl. He had lined up three more
on the arm of his chair, ready to eat
next.

Mum came in holding an open book in front of her. If I walk about reading books, I bump into the door-frame and hurt myself and she tells me off. I decided not to point this out to her.

"Auntie Annie next door has lent me this book. It's called, 'How to Choose the Best Instrument for Your Child to Learn to Play'."

"What's that book about?" asked Dan, sitting in the armchair, bits of orange all round his mouth.

Old Dan doesn't eat an orange politely. He doesn't pick out the bits they pack inside the peel and eat them one at a time. Dan just kind of peels off the top bit and then buries his mouth in the orange.

"What's the book about?!"

You see what I mean? Dan just asked HER that. What's the point of asking HIM the same thing?

"I don't know. What is the book about?"

"Well it's about choosing the right musical instrument for YOU. I need to start you on the right one and then you can pursue a musical career on that instrument for the rest of your life. This book tells me how to do that."

"Er?"

"Now, the saxophone you saw is no good for you, because it's too big and requires special breathing, and so forth. And in the hall there's an old banjo Auntie Annie's given you, but I've tried it and really it's past its best."

"It's busted," I suggested.

"Now Daniel, I've looked in the book to see what kind of instrument would suit a child like you, and it seems you should learn the piano. Would you like to learn to play the piano?"

"No thank you," Dan answered. "I'm eating a bazooka at the moment."

"Eating a bazooka?"

"It's a satsuma," I explained.

Well, if your own mother doesn't even know what a satsuma is...

"I'm just going to get something I've got for you, Ant. Don't go away for the moment."

"Shall we make a run for it?" I asked Dan, but Mum was already coming back in, carrying a long case.

Mum put the black case on the table and carefully took out an instrument.

"What is it?" Dan asked.

"What is it?! Don't YOU know what it is?"

"It's a violin," I told her.

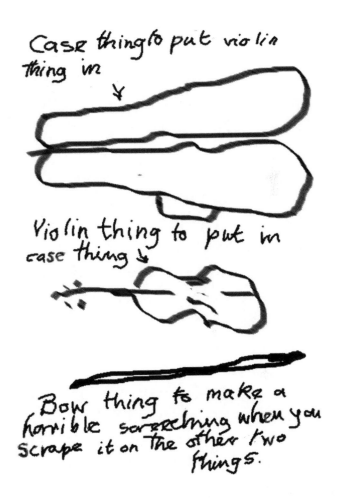

Case thing to put violin thing in

Violin thing to put in case thing

Bow thing to make a horrible screeching when you scrape it on the other two things.

Well, if your own mother doesn't even know what a violin is...

"According to the book, this is the right instrument for you, Ant.

Wouldn't you like to learn to play it?"

"No thank you," I said. "I'm just going to eat one of these satsumas, before Daniel gets to scoff that last one."

"Don't be silly," she insisted. "You'll love playing it. And once you've learnt to play it, you can give us all a beautiful concert. Come on, come here and I'll show you what you need to do."

I started to walk over to her, but she suddenly shouted: "Take that orange out of your mouth AT ONCE! And go and wash your hands this very minute, before you touch this beautiful instrument!"

I washed my hands the special rapid way where I don't need to use any soap. I just hold them in the water under the tap and rub them together a couple of times.

I went back in and held up my clean hands to Mum to show her, then I went to pick up the violin.

"Just a minute, what happened to the guitar we brought back from the shop? I need to put some new strings on it, to see if it will play."

"It's vanished," I said.

"It's mouldy," Dan said.

"Mouldy? Don't be silly. There's no mould on it at all."

"Mouldy doesn't mean it's mouldy," I said. "It means, we don't like it. It's rotten, and mad, sort of thing."

"I think you'd better tell me straight away where it is."

Mum sounded kind of menacing.

"It's a mystery," said Little Old Dan.

"Well you'd better find it soon, before I find you."

What does that mean? Mums are supposed to be able to make sense, aren't they?

I finally got to pick up the violin. Mum showed me how to put it under my chin and hold the bow thing. Then I had to scrape the bow thing across the cat's things.

I don't understand it either.

It made a wonderful noise: Squeaeaeaeaeaeaeaeaeeaeaeaeeaeek! Eeeeeeerraaaaaaaark! Eiiiiiiiii! Orrrrrrii! Aaiahhhk! Hhhieieieieik!

Dan and Mum had their fingers in their ears, squealing, "STOP! STOP! PLEASE STOP!"

Em bellowed down from upstairs, "Somebody stop him!"

I put the bow down and tried to speak with the violin under my chin. "Thank you Mum, I'm going to love playing the violin."

"That's what mouldy means," Dan said. "That was HORRIBLE, ROTTEN, MOULDY MUSIC!"

"Oh no," said Mum. "What HAVE I done?"

* * * *

You will find out just what Mum had done when you read the next book in the series. It's called, *Mouldy, Mad Concert*.
I just need to finish writing it.
After TV.
After my bath.
After bedtime.
After lights-out. Using a torch.

* * * *

If you have finished reading this book, PLEASE get your Mum, or your Dad, or your big, bad, mad sister, to write a REVIEW.

If I don't get any reviews, no one else will think it is worth reading the book.

If what we've got to call "The Reviewer" won't do it, or they keep forgetting to write a REVIEW, try asking them what each letter in the alphabet stands for, like this:

You: "What does A stand for?"

Mr. or Ms. X: "Alpha."

You: "What does B stand for?"

Mr. or Ms. X: "Bravo."

You: "What does C stand for?"

Of course, you should NEVER use blackmail. You will have to be nice. If it still doesn't work, or they say, "Yes Dear, I will, just as soon as I get a second to spare," then try mixing it up.

Suddenly ask this next: "What does Foxtrot stand for?"

If they can't get that right, you know you've got a serious problem.

＊ ＊ ＊ ＊

Me: "Mum, how do you spell
      'disclamation'?"

Mum:"Disclamation? Are you sure
      you've got that right?"

Me: "No Mum, I've got it wrong,
      so now I need to know how
      to spell it right."

Mum: "I've never heard of it. Ask
      your sister. She's the clever
      one round here."

Er? Madwoman Em, the clever one!
But I didn't dare say anything.
I crept up the stairs, opened her
door, and threw in my lined
notebook and pencil. When the
notebook didn't come flying back
out at me, I decided it was safe to go
in.

Em: "What do you want, my dear, beloved, little muppet?"

I picked up the notebook and pencil and took them across to her. I asked her how to spell 'disclamation' and she just kind of looked at me. Then she ignored the notebook but grabbed the pencil.

Em: "Now you see what you've done? This pencil is broken. Never throw a pencil, because the lead breaks."

Me: "Yes Em, but how do you spell it?"

Em: "There's no such word."

Me: "Yes, but if we did have the word, how would you spell it?"

Em: "With great difficulty, because THERE IS NO SUCH WORD!"

Me: "Yes, but ..."

Em: "All right, this is how you spell it, like this: F... A... T... H... E... A... D."

* * * *

6 DISCLAMATION MARK

No mosquitoes were hurt during the making of this story.

Signed: R. A. B. PRESIDENT OF THE NOWN UNIVERSE

Dan: "Em For said you put 'The Known Universe' on this bit of paper. Why do that?"

Me: "Because that's what they always put at the end of a film."

Em: "This isn't a film, Butthead."

Dan: "What is the unknown universe?"

Em: "If we knew that, it wouldn't be unknown, would it? You daft tune."

Me: "I don't know."

Em: "I'm telling you, aren't I? It's not a question."

Me: "I asked first."

Em: "What did you ask?"

Me: "I don't know."

Dan: "What other things don't we know?"

Em: "What other things don't we

know?!!!"

Me: "Dan just asked that."

Dan: "I don't know. What other
        things don't we know?"

Me: "A boy at school says that no
        one in the known world
        knows how to spell 'known'."

Em: "Well you certainly don't!
        Look how you've spelled it
        here, Zombie Features!
        You're supposed to use the
        spielchecker thing!"

Dan: "Who is President of The
        Unknown Universe?"

Em: "Who is President of the
        UNKNOWN UNIVERSE?!!"

Dan: "I don't know. Who is he?"

THE END

Ant_B

Other Children's Books By Robert Blanchett

Horrible Mouldy

This is the start of mouldiness. I call it -1 in the Mouldy Series. Emma calls it 'The Prequel', but no one knows what a prequel is.

The next mouldy book will be *Mouldy, Music, Concert*.

Younger Than You

This can be called "a semi-biographical collection of short stories", because that's what it is. The stories are based on Robert's childhood with his little brother, Terry.

33483914R00037

Printed in Great Britain
by Amazon